WAR IN THE JUNGLE

A New Orleans Urban Novel

AJ Bradford

authorHOUSE®

AuthorHouse™
1663 Liberty Drive
Bloomington, IN 47403
www.authorhouse.com
Phone: 1 (800) 839-8640

Published by AuthorHouse 03/19/2016

ISBN: 978-1-5049-8499-7 (sc)
ISBN: 978-1-5049-8498-0 (e)

Library of Congress Control Number: 2016904128

Print information available on the last page.

This book is printed on acid-free paper.

PROLOGUE

"YEAR 2010"

"One two three, one, one two three, two. Stretch it ladies, come on stretch it! The aerobics instructor yelled in a girl's high voice to his class in the Y.M.C.A. center.

All of the 12 females were on their knees in a doggy style position stretching their arms forward with their head touching the ground.

"Come on baby girl stretch that thing" Donnie told Rebecca he was right up on her rubbing against her butt with his hands pushing her back down acting like he's really trying to help her stretch.

"Damn this bitch got a soft ass" Donnie said to himself while getting up from behind Rebecca.

"Girl I think Donnie be lusting off us" Ashely told Jazzy.

"Don't worry about him girl because he is taking more dick than us" Jazzy responded back to Ashely, then they both bust out laughing.

"Alright ladies, this 45 minute class is over until tomorrow same time, same place," Donnie said while hitting Rebecca on her but telling her she did great.

"That's what I am talking about right there!" Ashely said pointing at what the instructor just did.

"He makes me wonder sometimes", Jazzy replied.

"Are you going to work today or is you taking off?" Ashely ask Jazzy while they were walking out the gym.

"I am off today, but I go back tomorrow because I got this guy who just been released from prison who I been evaluating for the last couple of months", Jazzy said.

"Is he crazy?" she ask.

"No girl he comes for therapy, he just needs someone to talk to."

"Is he handsome?" Ashely ask.

"Yeah, he's cute, smooth and very muscular", Jazzy said smiling.

"Um, um, um, Girl I know that look".

"What are you talking about?" Jazzy asked Ashely.

"Don't play mind games with the man, just be straight up if you are feeling him."

"Well you know I'm a psychologist, so I got to feel him out," Jazzy said.

"How long did he do in prison?"

"15 years", Jazzy responded.

"Girl if I wasn't married I'll want some of that jail house dick too." Ashely told Jazzy laughing.

"Girl you are a mess."

"Well Jazzy I will see you next week Ok", Ashely said while giving her a huge then jumped into her car and pulled off.

Before Jazzy got in her car she went into the trunk to get her Gucci glasses and sandals and changed out of her tennis shoes. On the other side of the parking lot two brothers Malcolm and Travis were heading into the Y.M.C.A. center to work out, but when they saw Jazzy bending over in the trunk of her blue 750 BMW. They stopped dead in their tracks.

"Damn dog, that girl got ass", Travis told his lil bro.

"Yeah you right, she look like Jessica Alba in that movie deep blue sea," Malcolm responded back to his brother.

"Naw, she favor that women with the red hair in transporter 3, the one who everybody was after remember"? Travis said.

"Yep she sure do bro."

Jazzy had a caramel skin complexion with freckles in her face. Red short hair, blue eyes, 5'6" in height, 140 lbs. in weight, all straight hips, thighs and cursed. Shorty had a body like pinky the vixen diva and she was Ms. Sophisticated.

When Jazzy got her glasses and sandals out the trunk, she seen them looking so she dropped her car keys on the ground making that ass clap together giving them on final performance.

"I know y'all wish y'all could have some of the milk shake" Jazzy said to herself.

"Hi guys", Jazzy said waving to them before jumping into the car.

"Hey....", they both said at the same time without blinking an eye thinking they might miss something.

When Jazzy started her car up she still had her CD player on blast playing, Lil lolly pop song from her sound system.

"Damn I would love to fuck the ship out that bitch!" Travis said as him and his brother was watching her car drive down the parking lot.

"Man you aint never lied and she didn't have on no draws with them tight ass gym shorts, Malcolm said while they both started walking up the stairs into the gym to work out.

While Jazzy was driving down the freeway she open the sun roof to the BMW to let her hair feel the breeze of the wind. When she pulled up to her condo in Eastover New Orleans, she saw that the paper boy had dropped off the new paper on the front porch. Soon as she got inside Jazzy put her gym bag on the sofa then went to turn on the shower while checking her answering machine.

You have one new message at 9:07 am beep. . . (Hi you have reach my voice mail either I'm busy or unavailable but if you leave your name, number and reason for your call, I promise to get back to you beep. . ., (hey Jazzy girl, this is your secretary Liza at the mental health department. I just wanted to remind you that Mr. Parkers appointment is at 1:00 pm today. That fine ass man with them big pretty eyes you know the one I'm talking about. Well if you aint coming in today, Let me know so I can reschedule him Ok, this is Liza, call me beep.

"Damn I thought his appointment was tomorrow"). Jazzy said to herself while taking her clothes off grabbing the shampoo stepping into the shower. She let the water rinse through her hair, shampoo suds' dripping all over her body. Jazzy felt so relaxed, the warm water was soften all the tension on her muscles. When she got out of the shower she dried off then walked into her bedroom butt naked looking at herself in the mirror.

"Damn I'm sexy", she said while rubbing on her tittles and ass.

Sher got dress putting on everything but no under wear and them spandex pants she had on made that ass jiggling baby! Grabbing her things heading out the door to work. When she got across the river to Jefferson Parish she took

Lolly pop CD out the player and put Alicia Keys disk in because they stereo type ya on this side of the river from what kind of music you listen to ya heard me! Once she made it to the mental health department, Jazzy parked her car then went into the lobby to the vending machines to buy a bottle water then got on the elevator to the seventy floor where her office was station.

"Hey girl, I though you wasn't coming in today", Liza told Jazzy soon as she entered the office.

"I though Mr. Parker was schedule for tomorrow", Jazzy replied.

"Nope, he on for today, damn girl is that the new Prada jean outfit?" Liza asked.

"Yep, from head to toe with the shoes to match," Jazzy said.

'Do your thing, I aint mad at ya dress to impress!, Mr. Parker is in the waiting room reading a magazine, do you want me to call him now?" Liza asked.

"Send him in about 30 minutes", Dr. Patterson told her secretary while walking into her office. Once she closed the door behind her she went into her desk drawer and put her prom picture on the desk table where it could be seen. She sprayed her blue berry perfume in the air while unbuttoning the top of her shirt, pushing her breasts up looking so seductive and putting on some pink lip gloss matching the color of her finger nails. According to Mr. Parker she was beautiful, irreplaceable everything he ever wanted (L.O.L.).

Knock, Knock, Knock . . .

"Come in ", Dr. Patterson said.

Soon as Mr. Parker entered her office taking a seat he couldn't help but notice that the scenery felt so different today.

"Hey . . . How are you doing today", she said smiling one of her many communication techniques.

"I'm doing OK but what's that tasteful smell?" Mr. Parker ask her.

"Oh, that's my body scent," she replied.

"Well I hope you feel how you look", he said while still making eye contact with her.

She blushed and smiled then said "thanks", playing that shy role.

"Did it hurt,?" he ask her.

"Did what hurt?" she responed.

"When you fell from heaven," he replied while still making eye contact with her.

"Yes it did matter of fact," she was wide open no and her pussy was soaking wet. Dr. Patterson wanted to give him some pussy right then and there but she got a hold of herself and changed the subject.

"What do you want to talk about today Mr. Parker because I thought your appointment was for tomorrow," she said.

"Well first of all, I been seeing you for a couple of months now, so you should have a feel of my character because I've shown you my cards so you know I'm not playing with you, feel me?"

"I feel you," she replied shaking her head like she was green.

"So what do you get from the conversations that we've been having," he asked her.

"You could be person s best friend or worst nightmare. It seems like it's hard for you to trust someone."

"So you been listening," he said.

"Why wouldn't I, it's my job then if I had done 15 years in prison and nobody was there for me. I would feel the same way too," Dr. Patterson said.

"That's what's up," he replied.

But I must say your life seems so exciting," she said.

"Yeah, I going to do this until it's over but it's far from over ya heard me, but what I want to talk about today is my son."

"You never mentioned anything about your son before," she said.

"Yeah I know because he's in prison with a life sentence but he is about to come home," Mr. Parker told Dr. Patterson.

"Well tell me the story you got my full attention," she said while putting her hands under her chin with elbows on the table leaning in making eye contact with them blue sparking eyes showing she really cared.

"Well sit back and enjoy this ride, because I'm bout to tell you a hell of a story so listen carefully," he told her.

CHAPTER 1

Cold World
June 13, 1988

Tonight was one of them nights where the homeless people wish they had air condition in their card board boxes under the bridge in the big easy. When the humility is very high with dry heat, no wind blowing and mosquitoes flying around your head. Everybody goes inside under the A.C. around 9:30 to 10:00 when there is a full moon above the cloud's because it get so much dry heat if you walk one block your clothes will start sticking to your body from the tempter that the humility admits down here in New Orleans ya heard me. It's so much dry heat, it makes you feel like you can't breathe but that was the last thing on...Donte and Omar's mind.

They was driving down North Causeway Blvd. Headed toward Metairie, Le.

"Man don't let that white Lexus out your sight!"...Donte told Omar.

They was following Mary home, Little Percy Sister was Cuban, a very attractive young women. Caramel skin complexion, long black hair, hazel eyes and she was a physical fitness trainer so you know her body was nice. She was 28 years of age with two daughters Melanie 8 and Myia 4 years of age. They was driving home from the super fair at the superdome. The kids were exhausted from running around having fun jumping on all the rides. The children still had the Kool aid stains on their clothes with the smell of cotton candy and candy apple on their breath. Mary was so happy just to see her girls having fun. She only wish her baby daddy Bill wasn't locked up in the feds, so he could enjoy this with them.

Little Percy never taught his sister how to play her review mirror to pay attention to see if anyone was following her let alone what he kept in her house. She always drove straight home taking no short cut or back streets to her house. Donte had her route down pack. This was his third time following Mary and she travel down the same road and turns and Donte knew it couldn't get no sweeter than this.

"Look homie, she's parking in front of the green and white house," Omar told Donte.

"Go park around the corner on the side street to give her enough time to get in the house, but remember this is a robbery not no murder," Donte responded back to Omar.

Mary jumped out the vehicle carrying 4 year old Myia while she was still sleeping and held 8 year old Melanie hand walking up he steps to her home. As she was trying to stick her key in the door in the dark, she remembers she forgot to change the light bulb over the front door so she could see but promise that she'll do it I in the morning because right now she was tried. When she finally unlocked the door, she walked in and closed the door behind her while bringing Melanie upstairs to her bed. The T.V. station was still on the cartoon channel but when Melanie seen Tom and Jerry her favorite cartoon, she sat on the sofa to watch it.

"Uncle Bob, Uncle Bob," Mary heard someone yelling while knocking on her door.

"Who the fuck is this knocking at my door talking about Uncle Bod," Mary said mobbing under her breath while walking fast down the steps to the door before they wake Myia up. She was about to tell the person on the other side of the door that they got the wrong house, but when she open the door and seen the looked in the eyes, she knew she made a mistake by opening the door. Donte busted into the house as soon as she opened the door knocking Mary to the ground while Omar hit her in the head with the butt of his gun and told her to be quite and follow instructions in a hype voice before he tied her hands and feet then picking her up putting her in a chair. Melanie was watching all of this with no fear in her eyes. A anger built up inside her that she never felt before and she didn't like what the masked men did to her mother. Omar tied her up as well then put duct tape on the kid's mouth so she wouldn't scream.

"Please don't hurt my babies," Mary said while crying softly sitting in the chair.

"Bitch where is the dope at?" Donte yelled at Mary.

"I'll give yall whatever you want, Please don't hurt us," she said.

"Bitch! Where's the drugs at," Donte said while pointing the gun to Melanie's head.

"I don't know what you are talking about, but I got 12, 000 dollars in my bedroom dresses, Please take it and leave."

"Oh bitch you think I'm playing, you think I'm stupid, Donte put the gun to little Melanie's head and cocked the gun.

"I don't know what you are talking about, please don't hurt my kinds," Mary was now yelling hoping somebody would hear her but Omar hit her again in the head with the butt of his gun them put duct tape around her mouth to stop her from making noise. Donte and Omar ram shacked her whole house. They found the 12,000 dollars she had in her dresses, but when they see little 4 year old Myia in her bed sleeping. They just looked at each other not knowing what to do. Omar picked the little girl up waking her out of her sleep to bring her into the living room with her tired up other and sister. Donte thought this was a blank mission until he kicked over the coffee table, But at the same time while Omar was sitting baby Myia down on the floor tying her feet. She pulled the band dander from around his face saying, "daddy, daddy" in a playing and happy voice while reaching for him to hold her. Mary, Melanie, Myia and ...Donte.. was now looking at his bare face.

Donte didn't want it to come to this but the decision had already been made. Donte picked up the 10 kilos of raw heroin out of the coffee table. Omar finished putting the duct tape around the baby's feet's, hands and mouth. He laid all three of them on their stomachs, put the silencer on the gun then shot them execution style killing Mary and baby Myia immediately while Melanie was just lying there still breathing. Omar mind was fucked up now. He was just staring at the kid body's laying there in a pool of blood until Donte pulled his arm toward the door to leave.

Donte thought that Omar wanted to kill them anyway. Omar was very stubborn, hard headed and rebellious. He was black as tart with a ball head, eyes cold as midnight, about `5 `9, weighed about 195 lbs. and he was extremely trigger happy with guns.

They were in the car driving back to New Orleans in silence. Omar was just sitting thinking why the kid had to pull off his band dander. He still had little Myia's memory in his head smiling, laughing calling him daddy. He never killed a kid before and that did worry him because he had a 4 year old daughter himself.

"Fuck . . .!" Omar said out shaking his head blaming his hand on the dash board.

Donte didn't know what was going on in Omars head, but he did feel his pain so he reached in the arm rest of the car and pulled out a fifth of Hennessey, popped it open and took a deep swallow and passed it to Omar. He grabbed the bottle and took two deep swallows, went into the glove department, grab a cigar and rolled a blunt. When Omar did look at Donte at the driving wheel, his eyes was smoking red before he took a puff off the gar. He nodded his head in agreement and they gave each other pound. A nightmare they would always remember. Donte turned the music on medium while they drove down interstate I-10 back to the Iberville projects with 10 bricks of raw heroin and 12,000 dollars.

Little Percy was standing in priority cemetery watching his family being put into the wall. A second line band was playing a sympathy song in the crowd standing along with the rest of Percy's family members. It was a dark cloudy day, wind blowing with a few light rain drops falling from the sky. Percy left the burial service and went sat in his black Cadillac car to think about who he had ever brought to his sister's house. The only sound you heard was the rain dropping onto the hood and roof of his car. The more he sat there, the more anger he got because he started feeling that he was responsible for Mary and Myia's death. He looked down at his phone than called one of the most respected street hustlers in New Orleans.

Ring, Ring, Ring . . . Ring, Ring, Ring . . .

"Hello, who that be like Whoddie," he said answering the phone.

"This Percy play boy".

"Hey . . . Percy very much unexpected call right?"

"Yeah, very much unexpected but very important, so listen close. Somebody or maybe I should say some animal shot my sister and her two daughters at her home last week", Tony informed him.

"Are they dead?"

"It don't matter if they are dead or not!"

"Whoever open a new dope spot with some raw dope? I got a nice reward out".

"hello?" percy said looking at the phone as if hand up.

"Yeah, Percy I'm still here and I heard every word you said so don't say no more. What don't need to be said shouldn't have to be explained because whoever trouble you, they trouble us ya heard me".

"I want everybody who had something to do with it, Mothers, Fathers, Kids and children! Cock suckers don't know who they are dealing with. I got a million to spend so if you want to cash in just play my lottery and hit jackpot,!" Percy said in an unforgettable voice before he hung up the phone.

Little Percy was a heavy drug lord and supplied 70% of the eastern region with heroin. He was very short with a fat stomach, slick hair hat he always combed to the right and he had a scar around his neck from an attempt on his life back in the 60s when he was in state prison. Percy was a very straight forward business man who wore suits and if you cop straight from him, he made sure you didn't spend your money nowhere else. But his only problem as a boss was that he put too much trust in this Cold world. Being loyal will get you very far but playing fair isn't always the element of being a true Wise Guy.

CHAPTER 2

"Girl here come Mitch duck ass, I bet he dnt got all ya money" shy told her best friend CupCake.

Im going to make that nigger eat this pussy." Cupcake respond back to shy.

"Fuck That"! His baby momma shanell shoundnt be always hating on a bitch just because she choose to live off the the walfare while im out here getting this dope money" cupcake told shy..

Bet not let that nigger put no dick in my pussy!" shy told cupcake in a demanding tone.

"Shy dnt start that shit, Im just getting at that hoe shanell." Cupcake said.

"wann.. whats up ya heard me. Are you straight shorty!? Mitch asked cupcake.

"Boy how much you got?" she asked

"Look I got 23 dollars, I give you two dollars tomorrow went I come back." Mitch told cupcake.

"Nigga you always coming short, plus all we got is 50 bags and im not bout to let you owe me shit unless you giving a lil lips and mouth services?" cupcake said with a devilish smile.

"Damn shorty"! you going to play ya boy like that.

"Nigger you aint my boy, you shanell boy!" she said rolling her eyes at him.

"Yall hoes out here in the lafeet projects thinking yall own this bitch and everybody in it huh?he said mad than a mother fucker.

"Say homie its cop or blow, so are you going to do because, A.T.F. be popping up out the blue on Tuesday and thurday ya heard me".shy told

"Where are we going to go because Im sure aint bout to go to no hotel im on my lunch break" he said.

"Nigga go into the abundant house rite there" cupcake told mitch.

"Girl they got them needles and stuff in there" mitch replyed.

"Nigga you want this bag of dope or not because you know its that raw dope in the city so stop playing and come suck this pussy before I change my mind!" cupcake said acting like she bout to walk out the abundant house.

"Alrite, alrite," But you bet not tell shanell and yall treating me like a junkie when this is my choice of drug. Bitch you lucky Im joneing rite now." mitch told cupcake.

Looking at the project building from the outside you'll think that somebody was living there. The building wasn't boarded up, instead it had blinds and certains on the inside and it was funish with two sofas, One black and white floor model Tv, a raido, and bed in the back room the spot to hide from the law to get high.

CupCake walked fast into the back room by the time mitch made it there. Cupcake was sitting on her sweater in the bed sitting up with her back against the Wall with her jeans off and her 38 slugg nose in her hand under the pillow.

"Damn girl, you like M.C. light, did anyone ever tell u that?" he ask her

"Yeah, all the time but come eat this pussy nigga."

"Let me shoot the dope first, then I could lick that thing for ya."

"Nope you aint bout to be noddling off before I get my nut." she said.

Mitch was anxious and fiending to shoot that dope so he said fuck it, butt he never ate pussy before at the age of 24. He though to just lick it like a lolly pop.

Soon as he started licking her pussy she knew he didn't know what he was doing, so she was guiding his head with her hands grinding into his face until he bite her pearl tounge not knowing what he did. She pushed his head back away and moaned in pain. Her pussy felt like a honey bee had stong it.

Mitch jumped up laughing saying "wheres my dope" Not knowing how much pain it caused her.

"Oh you think that shit funny nigga!"

She grab the 38 from under the pillow and shot Mitch three times in his forehead.

Shy heard the gun shots and ran into the room with her gun pulled out.

"Bitch what happen?" shy asked Cupcake.

"Dumb ass nigga bit my pearl tounge not knowing what he was doing then got the nerve to laugh!" Cupcake told shy while taking her time moving slow to put her leg back inside her jeans before she pulled them to her waist.

"Fuck him." Shy said than put two bags of dope besides his body before they left the building.

CHAPTER 3

"Damn we aint even get to the party yet, and you act like you are driving drunk." Cleve told Pretty.

"Naw homie it's the wheelor limement that I got to get fixed." Pretty responded back to Cleve.

"Man Im telling you dog, once we get a dope set. Thats millions of dollars." Pretty said.

"Nigga we doing good with this coke so what the fuck you talking bout?"

"The nigga Donte out the ville talking bout giving us a brick of raw for 70,000 ya heard me." Cleve told pretty.

Trill and wick was sitting in the back seat of the bronco just listing.

"Dog we dont got the whole 70 do we? Pretty asked?

"That's not the problems, dude talking bout giving it to us on consignment and its that raw!"

"Yeah!"

"Yeah man we could step on it and make two bricks feel me?" Cleve said

"If we sell all 50 bags we'll make every bit of 40,000 or more off each ounce, so you do the match." Wick said from the back seat.

Pretty looked thru the review mirror and said, “Damn its like everybody came to a understanding but me huh?”

“Stop trippin homie, we are just giving it to you now Yadig. It’s a win win situation, so lets get money.” Cleve said.

“We got to watch them dudes out the ville dog, this shit too sweet to be true.” pretty told Cleve.

“I say the same thing round.” Trill said.

“Its their party we are going to but if anything we’ll jack them fools feel me?” Cleve responed.

“That’s all I want to hear!” Trill said.

Its was just turning dark as they drove thru traffic on the highway. Pretty look up and seen the sign that said read blvd next exit so he switched lanes to dapart the interstate. While driving down Morrison ave. they pulled into the gas station to get some cigars. When pretty jumped back in the truck and before he had a chance to pull off. Two Mexicans driving a blue and sliver 87 boniville bump into the bronco breaking its tail light.

“Man what the fuck is these dudes stupid!” pretty said

All four of them jump out the truck.

“What all yall niggas jumping out the truck for?!” the drunking Mexican yelled.

Trill face turned red as a mother fucker.

“You right bruh, you got that” pretty said while giving everybody the signal to get back in the truck.

Lil Richard thought he had big nuts now as he seen the young men jump back into the black bronco. Lil Richard brother sam was scared as shit and he just knew it was going to be some trouble and his brother was in the wrong but when he seen they pulled off he was surprise.

“look bitch dnt trip, let me pull around the corner and you and wick go handle business, Me and Cleve going to be waiting!” pretty told trill in a demanding voice.

Trill smiled because he wanted to get at that wet back right then and there but pretty was smart enough not to get the truck on display. Trill and Wick put their band danners around their face, jump out the truck and ran behide the building to the gas station. The dump stubron ass Mexican was peeing on the this of the car while trying to pull gas. When they ran up on him and pointed the gun at his face, lil Richard looked trill in his eyes and said. "get the fuck out of here"

Those were the last words he ever spoke before he went to meet his maker. Trill shot him 6 times in his head with a 357 bulldog. His brother tried to jump out the car and run but wick tripped his feet leaving him to fall on his stomach.

"Turn over bitch"! Wick said.

"Im sorry, please dnt kill me!" sam was holding his hands over his face but 12 shots clicked his lights out.8 shots to the body and 4 to the head.

The clery in the gas station heard all the shots fired, but when she did pick up the phone to give the police a description of the murders, they was gone.

"Say homie you should have heard that wet back begging for his life, saying please dnt kill me Im sorry, Im sorry." Wick said mimicking the Mexican.

They all busted out laughing while passing the blunt around to smoke.

"I bet that Mexican wont talk shit to another Nigga." Pretty said while driving to the party like nothing never happen.

CHAPTER 4

"Damn girl my pussy is still hurting" Cupcake told shy.

"Bitch it only been 7 or 8 hours, your shit might be sore for a couple of days" shy reply

"Look at all them police cars over there at the gas station.I bet some young dumb ass boy robbed the place"

"Girl its that black paddle wagon so somebody got smoked." Cupcake said pointing at the two body bags marked off on the ground.

"Girl keep ya eyes on the rod before we crash because we're dirty as it is, Fuck whoever that is on the ground, bitch Im trying to get to this party to see which duck ass nigga we could trick and lick." Shy told Cupcake.

"Bitch this party is for them niggas out the Iberville." Cupcake said.

"Don't go acting funny on me now. This shit aint new to you, if you could put this pill in one of them niggas drinks then you know what time it is. Bitch all I see is money."

CupCake was just driving listing to shy words. She knew the drill and wasn't doing no trippin. They didn't play the club scene to much when they did, they rock niggas to sleep for everything because dumb ass dudes always think with their dick and get ass out.

When Cupcake pulled up in front the club. The line was crowed tailing around the block. You could hear the music blasting from inside everytime some one open the door at the enterence of the club. They had three security guards at the door trying to search people and made sure they didn't jump the line. The V.I.P. line was very short.

"Damn nigga how you going to charge me 125 dollars when you just let my sister pay you 100 dollars?!" she told the bouncer at the V.I.P. door.

Big sam been getting over all nite, but he seen this youngster wasn't going for it.

"It's a 100 dollars shorty what u talking bout?" big sam told the young lady.

"Oh dnt be trying to play me." She said while paying him then walked into the club.

Big sam started laughing then closed the door behide her.

"Is that 4th ward in the house tonight." The DJ yelled to the crowd from on the stage.

"Is that 6th ward in the house tonight?" hell…. Yeah! The crowd responed.

"Oh oo…, that 4th ward," "oo…, that 7th ward," "oh oo…, that 5th ward." The crowd started yelling out their hoods.

"I see downtown is running this bitch tonight" the DJ yelled thru the mic, "but I want to give a shout out to all my niggas out the ville ya heard me" wannnn.!

"Man this bitch warren got the club jumping huh bruh," tuna told ken as they was sitting on the bar stand drinking Hennessey.

"Damn who them two broads are right there?" Ken ask while pointing at the two females as they walked into the club.

"I know Im feeling shorty style and she rocking that jeanfit with them travel fox shoes on." tuna said.

"She must got a few dollars with that big ass hairebone chain and hoops earrings." Ken replyed.

"Look they are coming to the bar, I got shorty dnt trip, you take her girl slim." Tuna told ken.

"Bitch aint that them niggas out the ville right there sitting at the bar?" shy asked Cupcake.

"Yeah I believe so" Cupcake reply.

"You know what time it is to the bar with go." Shy said while they headed to the bar to catch their prey.

Cupcake made sure she sat on the side right next to Tuna. She seen him eyeing her so she knew he was a victim. While sitting down she looked him up and down rolling her eyes than started waving her hand to the bar tender to get her and shy two drinks. Tuna seen this was a pefect opportunity to make his move on shorty. He got me Tammie attention and order two drinks for Cupcake and Shy.

"Oh I guess you are a baller huh, with that saints starter jacket and addis form on." Cupcake told him.

"My name is tuna and I just want to know if I can have ya autograph because Im your biggest fan." Tuna told Cupcake.

"So I see you got game huh, and thanks for the drinks" she said while dropping a 100 dollar bill on the floor next to tuna chair.

"whats your name shorty?"

"What I cant hear you speak up!"

"Whats your name!" tuna yelled out loud and slow over the loud music.

"My name is Cupcake" she replyed while pointing to the ground, so tuna could look down and pick up the money.

Soon as he bent down to pick the money up, she eased two drops of visen into his drink.

"I guess that's your huh?" she asked him.

"Naw cupcake, its not mines, because I got all 50 dollars bills ya heard me so take it you might need it more than me so count it as a blessing." Tuna told her.

"Naw dude I got money!"

"Well you sure do look like it" he said.

"Let make a toast to that" tuna said but before he had the chance to take a drink.

Omar came throw the crowd to stop him.

"Bitch we got a meeting up stairs in the pool room" Omar told tuna while giving Cupcake the evil eye.

"Are them niggas out the Bernard here yet?" tuna asked Omar.

"Yeah everybody is up stairs waiting on you and ken, so lets go and give that drink to someone because we got to take care of business."

"Give me a minute cupcake, I will be rite back" tuna told her while leaveing his drink on the bar. Soon as he left a waitress was coming to the bar to order rounds of drinks but when she seen him put his cup on the table to leave she grabbed his arm.

"Excuse me sir, but you are leaving your drink" the waitress said.

"Take it to the head baby, that one on me." Tuna told her while him, ken and omar dip thru the crowd to the up stairs pool room.

She drunk it with one swallow than waved the bar tender down to order more drinks for the dancers who was preforming.

Donte was still watching shy and cupcake from behind the tinted glass up stairs in the pool room. When the bounder let ken omar and tuna into the pool room Donte informed tuna that the two females at the bar was trying to kinnapp and rob him.

"Man you trippin Donte" what make you think something like that?" tuna asked.

"I know both of their M.O. the one you was talking to name is cupcake and the other one name is shy. They from the lafeet projects. When you bended down to get watever you got from off the floor. She put something into your drink ya heaed me" Donte told tuna.

"Yeah!" he replyed

"Man Im telling you I been watching yall the whole time, but dnt trip we could use them as apart of our plot because they pump that dope too, so dnt trip feel me?"

"Look them niggas out the Bernard is in the back watching them strippers shoot pool, so get focus dnt trip." Donte told tuna while they was walking to the back of the pool room.

The pool room was at the top of the club with tinted see thru widows where the people on the outside couldn't see in or knew who was watching them. This area of the club had white and green marble floors, three round connected green letha sofas. A long and wide round table, two pool tables, D.J booth with red and green lights spinning around from the sealing with a couple of rappers pictures on the wall.

This was a V.I.P. section but since Donte was investing his money into this club he had different plans.

"Wannnn....baby" Donte greeted pretty, Cleve and the rest of his homies once they sat at the round table while puffing on a nine inch mardi gras cigar packed with a ounce of indoor weed.

"Man I always wanted to do that" pretty said pointing at the cigar.

As the gar was being pass around now it was time to talk business.

"Well like I told you once before Cleve, I like how you and your click is holding it down back there in the St. Bernard. I know from ya reputation that you dnt play games, but is you trying to jump on borad with this dope money forsure money?" Donte asked Cleve while putting a brick of herion on the table.

Trill eyes got big when he seen the dope on the table. He wish he had his gun to shoot all of them and take the dope, but they was patted down before they was allowed into the pool room.

"How much cut can it take again?" Cleve ask Donte.

"It can take a 5 but if I was you, I would put a three to keep the dope pure ya heard me" he replyed.

"That's like three bricks for the price of one." Cleve said out loud.

"This time I'll give it to you for 100,000 co-signment but next time C.O.D. feel me?"

"Dnt trip Donte we got ya, but I got one question. What made yall pick us?" Cleve asked donte.

"Personally I could give a fuck about ya, but professionally lets get back to the money" Donte said.

"real talk paly boy you aint saying nothing ya heard me" cleve said.

"And remember Cleve I cant lose because I got the whole city behind me, so dnt cross me" Donte said then slip the brick of dope arcoss the table to pretty who was sitting beside Cleve.

Everybody heard the music stop playing in the club while the DJ was on the mic telling the crowd to back up give her some space to breathe.

Donte, Omar and ken and everybody else in the pool room went to look out the glass into the club to see what the fuck was going on out there. Donte and tuna already knew what the problem was. It was the waitress who drunk the visen in tuna Hennessey. She was shaking forming from the mouth. Tuna and donte just looked at each other saking their heads watching the bounder take the waitress out the side door uncase she die, at least it wont be inside the club and that was the only concern the owner big mike had in mind. Once she was out the club everything went back to normal and the DJ started back playing the music like nothing never happen.

"Say homie, we are out yadig" Cleve told donte.

"Look went yall are done page this number and I'll have one of my people pick it up and we'll go from there ya heard me" Donte told Cleve while handing him a beeper number.

"say nomore" Cleve said while they all shoke hands and hugged each other before Cleve, pretty and trill left the party.

"Bitch everything is falling into place feel me?" Donte told tuna and omar.

"Look in the corner over there" Omar pointed to Cupcake trying to work big dee from uptown.

"Now its on you tuna toput some dope in the lafeet projects but you got to make that bitch think its all good ya heard" Donte told him.

"I got her dnt trip yall watch my work" tuna said before he went into the club to get at Cupcake.

As tuna was walking thru the crowd Cupcake and big dee was on side of the pacman machaine laughing until tuna walked up.

"damn shorty I told you I'll be rite back" tuna told her.

"My bad homie, I didn't know shorty was ya people. Look Im out" big dee said while dipping thru the crowd.

"He act like he was sure damn scared of you" Cupcake told tuna while looking him up and down from head to toe.

"Nigga know I put the house up behind all my hoes" tuna said.

"so Im ya hoe now huh?" she replyed.

"Naw you my dog cupcake so stop trippin.im bout my money and from the way you dress, I see you are too!" he said.

"If it dnt make dollars it dnt mak cents ya heard me" she responed

"What do you hustle or something?" he asked.

"I do a little something why?"

"I got this last 63 grams of raw dope im trying to get off."

"How much do you want for it?" she said.

"For you just give me 15,000."

"How much cut can it take?" she asked.

"It can take a 5" he repled.

"A 5!"

"Yeah a 5, but I need the money tonight if you got it or can go get it" tuna told cupcake.

"nigga you aint saying nothing!" she said while walking thru the crowd to the bar to get shy.

"Bitch! Guess what?" cupcake said to shy.

"What the fuck is you all excited for?" shy responed.

"the nigger out the ville tuna is talking bout he got 63 grams of raw for 15,000 that cn take a 5!" she told shy.

"damn what made you tell dude you sell dope?" she asked her.

"I didn't tell him anything, he just offered it. Dude talking bout he like my style."

"Bitch you are not sticking to the strip. We didn't come here to make a business deal and it seem strange that he come out the blue and offer you that." Shy said.

"what you think he seem the waitress on the floor after she drunk his drink?" cupcake asked shy.

"I dnt know but bitch you are trippin and slippin"

"just trust me for once, Im going to work him for everything he got!" Cupcake told shy while they was walking out the club to go get that money.

CHAPTER 5

Dope
Money, For Sure Money

"How much you got homie," Trill asked the friend while holding a chopper in his hand.

"I got 25 dollars and why yall got them big ass guns out here?" he ask.

Trill didn't bother to answer, but told him to wait until dude came out before he went into the hallway.

Trill was down stairs on the ground on side of the project building directing the dope sells to the hallway. Wick was on the first floor taking the money while Pretty was on the second floor with a chopper safe guarding Bull while he was making all the hand to hand sells transaction with the friends. It was about 2:45 am when Cleve pulled up on Mintion and Floy Park Court way in the St. Bernard projects. Soon as he looked down the court way it had to be about 100 people he seen down up waiting to get their fix.

"This is what the fuck I'm talking bout!" Cleve said while jumping out the SUV with all black on.

"Hold the rest of them at the bottom of the stairs so I could go get three more bundles right Quick," Bull told Pretty.

"Bitch! Hurry up, it's a rust out here!" Pretty told Bull while he went into the apartment to get more dope.

Within the last 45 minutes they sold about seven G bundles and now Bull as going to get three more ya dig. Ten stacks in an hour and a half ya heard me! NO MONEY LIKE DOPE MONEY!!!

Meanwhile back in the project...Donte..and Omar was just chillin.

"Man where the fuck this bitch sandman at,"...Donte.. asked Omar.

"I don't know where that nigga at, but he know too much," Omar replied.

"Yeah you right then you know that was his sister in law and two nieces. I promised that it was going to be a robbery not no murder, but it is what it is. I still got his cut from putting us on the lick,"...Donte..told Omar.

"Well you know what time it is when we do catch him," Omar replied.

Donte didn't say anything while he was puffing off a blunt in Sam's Store parking lot on Conti and Villere.

Sandman was Bill little brother, but after Bill got sentence to 30 years in the feds. Sandman fucked up the last remaining money Bill did have and little Percy knew too. Percy called him a slime ball, a straight fuck up. Sandman knew Percy kept some drugs in Mary's house but he didn't know how much. He just wanted some money so he made... Donte..promise that they was only going to take the drugs without hurting them. Nobody would ever know not Percy or Mary end of story but when he heard that Mary, Myia was killed and Melanie was shot in the head but was still living.

He didn't know what to do or say. All he kept saying to his self was that he promised a safe robbery not no murder! He didn't know if he should tell his brother or Percy what he did but he knew they both would wish death on him so he came to the conclusion to call...Donte..to see how much money he had waiting for him.

Ringing of a phone. . .Ring . . . Ring. . .

"What . . .,"...Donte..said answering his phone.

"What's up man this is Sandman, I'm trying to come see how much money you got for me," he said.

Donte hit Omar on the arm pointing at the phone letting him know that Sandman was on the phone.

"Man I been trying to get in touch with you for the last couple of days. What you went on vacation or something?" ...Donte..asked Sandman.

"Yeah man, I needed a peace of mind but now I need some money to pay the bills so I know you got something nice for me," Sandman said.

"I got you love just meet me back in the St. Bernard about 9:30 tonight feel me,"...Donte..said.

"I feel ya dog," he said then hung up the phone.

He didnt even see it coming. "Close Casket"

CHAPTER 6

"Yo, Cupcake I'm sick, ya heard me," a dope fiend told here while walking towards her holding her stomach.

"I'm all out now Slim, you should have come a little earlier," she told him.

"Come on baby girl, don't do me like that," he said then started throwing up the little food he had on his stomach.

"Girl let's get off the set before these dope fiends stat tripping thinking we're lying to them and I hate to see them like that," Shy told Cupcake while jumping in a white Corvette.

"I heard them niggas out the St. Bernard got the same dope we got," Shy told Cupcake.

"They might be fucking with them niggas out the Ville too, but they only open shop from 1:00 to 6:00 pm for what I heard," Cupcake said.

"As of now they aint messing with our money, but you got to get that nigga Tuna to take you to the stash spot. Bitch you say the nigga is feeling your style huh?" Cupcake ask.

"Yeah I got this, but let's dip through the Iberville to see if these dudes is out," Cupcake said.

They pulled up on Cozet and Bienville Street in front of the store then jumped out.

"Yall seen Tuna?" Cupcake asked the corner hustler's.

"Damn shorty! You finer than a mother fucker," the youngest told Cupcake.

"How old are you young'un?" she asked him.

"I'm 13 years old but age aint nothing but a number and my name is Bud," he said.

"Alright Bud, I like your attitude but what you got out here."

"I got 50 dollars ounces of the indoor," Bud told her.

"Check this Bud, take this 100 dollar bill and when you see Tuna come around let him know Cupcake is trying to see him," she said.

"Fuck that nigga Cupcake! I'm trying to fuck something so what's up?" Little Bud pressed her.

Shy and Cupcake both busted out laughing while jumping in the can then pulled off.

Little Percy was in Miami on his speed boat catching a sun tan laying on his back relaxing enjoying the good Florida weather. It was a very beautiful day in the sunshine state. Clear blue water with the dolphins playing around jumping in and out of the water. Percy was feeling himself until his mobile roller phone rang.

"Hello. . ." Percy said.

"What . . . my man,"...Donte..said from the other end of the phone.

"What's up baby, tell me something good," Percy said.

"Some dudes out the St. Bernard projects got a new dope set popping and two female's out the Lafitte projects in on too,"...Donte..told Percy.

"Is that right?"

"Yep that's right, I told you I got ya Percy. Your beef is my beef ya heard me."

"You have my blessing baby boy so get money," Percy told Donte.

"Yeah, them dumb ass dudes out the Bernard talking bout how easy it was to jack a Cuban for ten bricks. . .

"Wait, wait, wait a minute," Percy said in a clam cool but collective voce because he knew he never told nobody how much dope was missing from his sister house and now this dude is saying more info than what's out there.

"Don't worry, don't worry man. I'm sending you my personal blessing, so enjoy," Percy told...Donte..before hanging up the phone.

Little Percy leaned over and grab his rolled up 100 dollar bill and sniffed three lines of that dope then took a long swallow from his Hennessey bottle before laying back going into a firer nodded. Percy didn't give a fuck but long as mother fuckers was dying blood being spilled besides something he created, that's all that matter. All the pieces was coming together now and he knew Sandman death had something to do with his sister but just couldn't put his hands on it.

Percy was caught off guard as the F.B.I. surrounded him in their police boats. The two naked Cuban females ran down to the bottom of the boat to put their clothes back on because the party was over, ya heard me.

"Put your hands up where I can see them!" the F.B.I. agent yelled while the rest of them had their guns pointed at Percy.

Percy leaned up and took another snip of the dope because he knew that the Feds had to have something on him.

"Holiday Inn Hotel"

"Everything is coming together now baby, I told you this is a win - win situation," Pretty told Cleve.

"Yep, something like that," he replied.

"Man fuck them niggas! Let's jack them for everything," Wick busted out and said.

"Be cool baby, be cool only in due time, but we can't bite the hand that's feeding us?" Pretty ask out loud.

Everybody in the hotel got quite and didn't say anything. Trill and Bull was in the corner bust counting the 100,000 they was bout to drop off to...Donte..

"Man I still don't trust them dudes and why they want all of us to come to the meeting!" Wick asked Pretty in a demanding voice.

"Damn homie! Clam the fuck down can't you see we are winning right now," Pretty told Wick.

"Check this out," Wick said out loud," I'm chilling I'm the hotel until yall get back then you tell me what happen, but other than that I'm cooling."

"Yall ready?" Cleve ask Bull and Trill.

"Yep, it's all here," Bull responded.

Pretty, Trill, Cleve and Bull left the holiday Inn Hotel in a blue Astor van to meet...Donte..with his money. As they were driving down Bienville Street they mad a left turn on Tonti Street and parked in front of the yellow and white house but from the looks of it, it looked abandon.

"Man what time is it?" Cleve ask.

"It's a quarter to nine," Pretty replied.

It was already dark with nobody in sight. Even the cats and dogs didn't hang out in this area. Soon as Pretty turn the engine off to take the keys out the ignition, a U-Haul truck pulled up right alongside them to block them in. Two masked men jumped out of the U-Haul in all black with them choppers in their hands ya heard me. The first shot hit Pretty in his neck. Blood spilled all on the windshield and the dash board. They all was caught off guard so their first reaction was to duck down on the floor of the van, but that didn't help. The two masked men was right up beside the driver window and back seat letting multiple rounds inside the van. They both had 100 round clips on them choppers so every bullet went in their lifeless bodies. One masked gunmen jumps on the hood of the van letting off 30 shots inside after he went inside the van to grab a bag of blood money, ya heard me and that was all you seen but nothing but gun smoke nothing but gun smoke.

Meanwhile

Wick had just awaken from a two hour nap. When he got up the first thing he did was light a blunt.

"Dame I got a headache," he said.

Soon as he started puffing off the gar he got a sharp pain in his chest. He got off the bed to get his asthmas pump out his jacket pocked because he never felt like this before. As he sprayed the pump into his mouth he still didn't feel right. He walked over to the T.V. station to put the videos on channel 10 the box video station but as he was changing through the channels, he saw that 4 people been killed all at one time in a blue Astro Van. He was watching the 12:00am news on channel 4 W.W.L. the news commentator was giving a brief description of the topics for the morning. Once they came back from commercial Wick turned up the volume.

("Hi my name is Tracy smallwoods here at channel 4 news. They had a multiple homicide right her on Bienville and Tonti Street. It has been said that the unidentified victims were 4 males in their late 20s. As you can see here, it's about 100 and counting bullet shells on the ground marked by the orange cones. The victims were found with three pistols, bullet proof vest and weed inside the van so we believe this was drug related. At this time we have no leads or suspects if anyone has any information please call crime stopper the number is at the bottom of the screen. This is Tracy here at channel 4 news back to you Rick," she said.)

Wick was just sitting there on the bed with tears coming down his face. He already knew what time it was. His heart was black as tar. He cut the T.V. off and went into the dresser drawer to get his 40 cal pistol. When he looked on the night stand there was a fifth of Hennessey that had never been open. He grabbed the bottle and pop the top.

"I swear my nigga on everything I love I'm going to get them bitch niggas and keep getting this money," he said before he downed the whole bottle of Hennessey.

CHAPTER 7

"It's Going Down"

Ringing of a phone. Ring . . . ring . . . ring . . .

"Hello!" Cupcake said as she was turning the volume down on her car radio.

"Bitch! Where are you?" She asked Cupcake.

"I'm on my way from the Dillard Shopping Center, why girl what's good?" she ask.

"I know you seen the news this morning about them 4 dudes getting killed in the van last night?" She asked her.

"No girl, I didn't watch it but who was they and where did it happen at?" Cupcake replied.

"I think it was somewhere across Board on Bienville Street and everybody saying that was them niggas from the St. Bernard projects."

"Yeah!" Cupcake responded.

"Yep, and them niggas had some coke and some guns in the van with them so you know the news people was talking about it could be drug related."

"I don't know what they was doing with all that money with them but all their customers will be coming to us." Cupcake told Shy.

"What's up with dude anyway, have he got back at ya yet?"

"Not yet but I'm about to call his phone now. Look I'm coming down the Claiborne Bridge now. I'll let you know what he said when I pull up back there in the projects Ok." Cupcake told Shy.

"When you come back here I'm on Orleans and Galves Street the Chinese store ya heard me."

"I heard ya," Cupcake responded hanging up the phone.

"I hope this bitch nigga answer his phone," Cupcake said before she dial Tuna cell number.

"Ringing of a phone, Ring . . . ring . . . ring. . ."

"Wha. . .who- da be like who-dat?" Tuna said answering his phone.

"Damn nigga I been paging you for the last two days, but what's really good ya-dig," Cupcake told Tuna.

"Who is this?" he replied.

"Boy this Cupcake."

"Oh my bad shorty. I dint recognize your voice for a minute. I lost my paper so that's why I haven't hit you back but I thought for a minute since you didn't call, you wanted to make this only business and not pleasure," Tuna told Cupcake nice, smooth and easy.

"Um, a bitch like me want the best of both worlds feel me?" she said.

"Shit, you I feel ya but you don't need no money shorty I got you personally and professionally ya dig."

"You sure do know how to make a bitch pussy wet huh," she told him.

"Give me the opportunity and I could make your mouth wet, Tuna said so seductively.

"And you got jokes," she said.

"Shorty I'm dead serious," he said. Look meet me in the lobby at the Holiday Inn Hotel on Canal and Claiborne Street in 30 minutes," Tuna told Cupcake.

"Alright dude, I'll see you then," she said before hanging up the phone to call Shy.

"Hello." Shy said answering the phone.

"Bitch I got him!"

"Girl what the fuck is you talking bout?" Shy asked her.

"I'm on my way to meet dude at the Holiday Inn on Canal and Claiborne Street so when I know the room number, I'll page it to you on your beeper," Cupcake told Shy.

"Bitch try to put some pills in his drink before you page me, but if you can't just put 4444 beside the room number so I'll know how to prepared and be careful because word on the streets is them niggas is responsible for killing them boy zot the St. Bernard in the van, ya heard me," Shy informed her.

"I heard ya, but we are bout to get this duck ass nigga for whatever he got," Cupcake said.

"I know you got that tool on you right?" Shy asked her.

"Bitch I keep this three sight cocked!"

"Alright girl work your magic and know that I'm bringing lil-Tim and Q-lee." Shy told her before they hung up the phone.

As Cupcake was pulling up in the hotel parking lot she got a bad feeling bout this one, but she knew this nigga has at least a brick of heroin somewhere and now she was about to find out.

Tuna already had a room in the Holiday Inn for about three weeks. A room just for fucking bitch'zies and the room was in a fiends name, so he had plans to dome check Cupcake soon as they got into the room together. Soon as

Tuna walked in the lobby he didn't see Cupcake so he called her phone.

"Hello," she answered the phone.

"Where are you shorty," "I'm standing in the lobby now what's up?" he said.

"Look I'm in the parking lot just give me a few seconds, I'm on my way," she said then hung up.

When she walked in the lobby she really seen how handsome Tuna was so she had a big Kool aid smile on her face and so did he. They walked out the lobby up the stairs holding hands like a perfect couple on a beautiful date. Cupcake and Tuna came walking down the hallway arm in arm like a perfect couple. Tuna had his left hand massaging Cupcakes right ass cheek. Her booty was so soft that it felt like a squeeze. When they stopped in front the door, Cupcake started grinding on Tunas manhood. Tuna knew she had some good pussy so he wanted to fuck the shit out of her before he kill her. Cupcakes had one thing on her mind and that was to rob this nigga for everything h had by all means necessary. Soon as they enter the room she jump on Tuna propping her legs around his waist. Tuna carried her to the bed while tongue kissing her. They had a big mirror against the wall next to the bed and Tuna couldn't wait to watch himself pound in and out of that ass, ya hear me. Cupcake laid back on the bed while lifting her mini skirt to her waist spreading her legs wide open thinking Tuna was going to eat her pussy but she had another thing coming. Tuna turned her over man handling her putting her in a doggy style position while unzipping his jeans dropping his boxers putting two hands on her ass easing into Cupcakes virginal slowly.

"Ah," Cupcake moaned softly.

She started moving her ass side to side trying to help Tuna ease inside her wet tight pussy without hurting her. She had her head laid sideways on the pillow looking into the mirror making all kind of faces. Tuna was watching in the mirror also enjoying every moment of her pussy slow rolling that thing. Soon at that pussy started opening up Tuna started moving faster and faster and Cupcake started moaning louder and louder. Just that fast Tuna forgot about the mission at hand. He pulled out of her and nutted all on her ass cheeks while wiping his dick head all between her butt.

"Damn shorty this is the best pussy that I ever had," he told her in a so relaxed mode.

"Hold up Imp not finish with you," she replied while sitting him on the bed while she goes on all fours to give him some head.

She massaging his manhood back hard then started sobbing up and down side to side making sure he felt ever bit of her tongue right. Tuna started moaning, as she watched his facial expressions. His eyes started rolling behind his head so she pushed his chest back encouraging him to lay back on the bed to enjoy. She took it out her mouth and gave his balls some affection then put Mr. Willison back in her mouth. He busted off all in her mouth and she swallow every bit of it knowing this was a hell of a pay day. When she eased to her get three out of her boobs, someone knocked hard on the door.

Knock . . . knock. . Knock. . .

"Security room service! Please open the door," one of the two security guards said.

Knock . . . knock . . . knock . . .

"Security room service!" they said in a loud tone of voice, wearing all black suits with ear pieced and hand walkie talkies in their hands.

Tuna jumped up spooking thinking about all the money he had in the room. He pulled his pants up telling Cupcake to be cool before he stepped outside in the hallway. When he open the door they was trying to look in but Tuna closed the door behind him.

"What's up with you two big guys, how could I help y'all?" Tuna asked while guarding the door.

"My name is Peter and this is my partner Bob. We are the security of this hotel. For the last several days we been getting a lot of complains about a lot of loud sounds from females in this room," Peter told Tuna acting like some investigators on C.S.I. Miami.

"Well sir as you can see," Tuna cracked the door letting them see Cupcake sitting on the bed with her legs wide open smiling at them then closed the door back. "I'm here with many of one of my lady friends doing what two grown people love doing when they are madly in love feel me? Let me tell y'all a secret," Tuna said in a low voice informing them to come closer. "Man this bitch got the best pussy I ever had in my life and do you want to know something else?"

Both of them was interested in the details. They both looked at each other wanting to know more.

"Man she suck dick good too and she swallow it," Tuna told them.

"Yeah!" they both said at the same time.

While Tuna was entertaining the security guard from not coming in the room Cupcake knew it was game time. She started searching the room for any drugs or money. This damn room was filled with new clothes and shoes all over with shopping bags ever where. When she looked under the bed, she saw a black book sack. When she pulled the bag from under the bed she got butterflies not knowing if Tuna was about to walk right back into the room. Soon as she open the bag it was filled with stacks of 20s, 50s, and 100 dollar bills wrapped with brown rubber bands.

"Jackpot!" she said to herself.

When she looked at the door she heard Tuna outside laughing with the guards about who knows what then she looked at the window. Her heart was pumping fast not knowing if she should blaze this nigga when he come back into the room or hit the window down the fire escape. She knew she had to come to a decision fast but when she heard the first gun shot out in the hallway. Her body made up her mind for her and she was out the window down the fire escape stairs with the black book sack on her back running through the parking lot as she jumped into her corvette and burned rubber down Claiborne Ave.

Wick can't believe what he was seeing after turning down the hallway heading to the elevator. It was one of them niggas from the Iberville standing there talking and laughing with two hotel security guards like three child hood friends who haven't see each other in years. A whole burden just been lifted off of Wick back. He felt so good when he pulled the trigger letting off multiple rounds down the hallway at Tuna and everybody else who was in the way. The first shot hit Bob in the neck causing him to fall to the ground immediately grasping for air. Out of shock Tuna jumped behind Peter using his as a human shield as Peter pulled his gun turning his head with one hand over his face while shooting back. Tuna didn't know what the fuck was going on until he felt the air of a bullet passing onside of his head. That's when he realized he needed to catch some shelter. He ran back into his room closing the door behind him leaving Peter to fight for himself but. As he went to his jacket to get his gun, he noticed that the window was wide open with the curtains blowing from the wind. That's when he remembered Cupcake was in the room with him. The first place he looked was under the bed checking to see if the black book sack was still there, but when he saw it was goon, he wasn't tripping he had to focus on the matter at hand. When he looked at the door he heard the shooting stop. When he opened the door with his gun aimed and cocked, he saw several other doors open looking into the hallway to see what happen.

"Help me man please help me," Peter the security guard was reaching out his hand for Tuna to help him, but Tuna closed the door back and headed out the window down the stairs

CHAPTER 8

"Charity Hospital, A.K.A. The City Zoo!!!"

On October 14, 1988 about 3:37 in the morning, Tiddy baby was in the hospital about to have her baby boy. She was so happy that this was about to be over. ...Donte..her baby daddy was right there by her side trying to comfort her the best way he could, but the words that was coming out his mouth meant nothing to her. All she heard was "push baby push," before she passed out. Doctor Jones immediately called for surgery, Tiddy baby needed a C-section.

"Excuse me Mr. Parker, but this is going to be real ugly scene so if you want to step out, I'll advise you this is now," Dr. Jones told Donte.

"Lady you wouldn't believe how many dead bodies I have seen. This is my family Ms. Jones and I want to be by their side every step of the way,"...Donte..responded back to the doctor of the best.

Printed in the United States
By Bookmasters